The Journey of Odysseus

Written by Hawys Morgan
Illustrated by Martin Bustamante

Collins

Introduction

I'm Odysseus, King of Ithaca. For ten years, my Greek warriors and I fought and won many bloody battles over the seas in Troy.

It was time for us to return home, victorious.

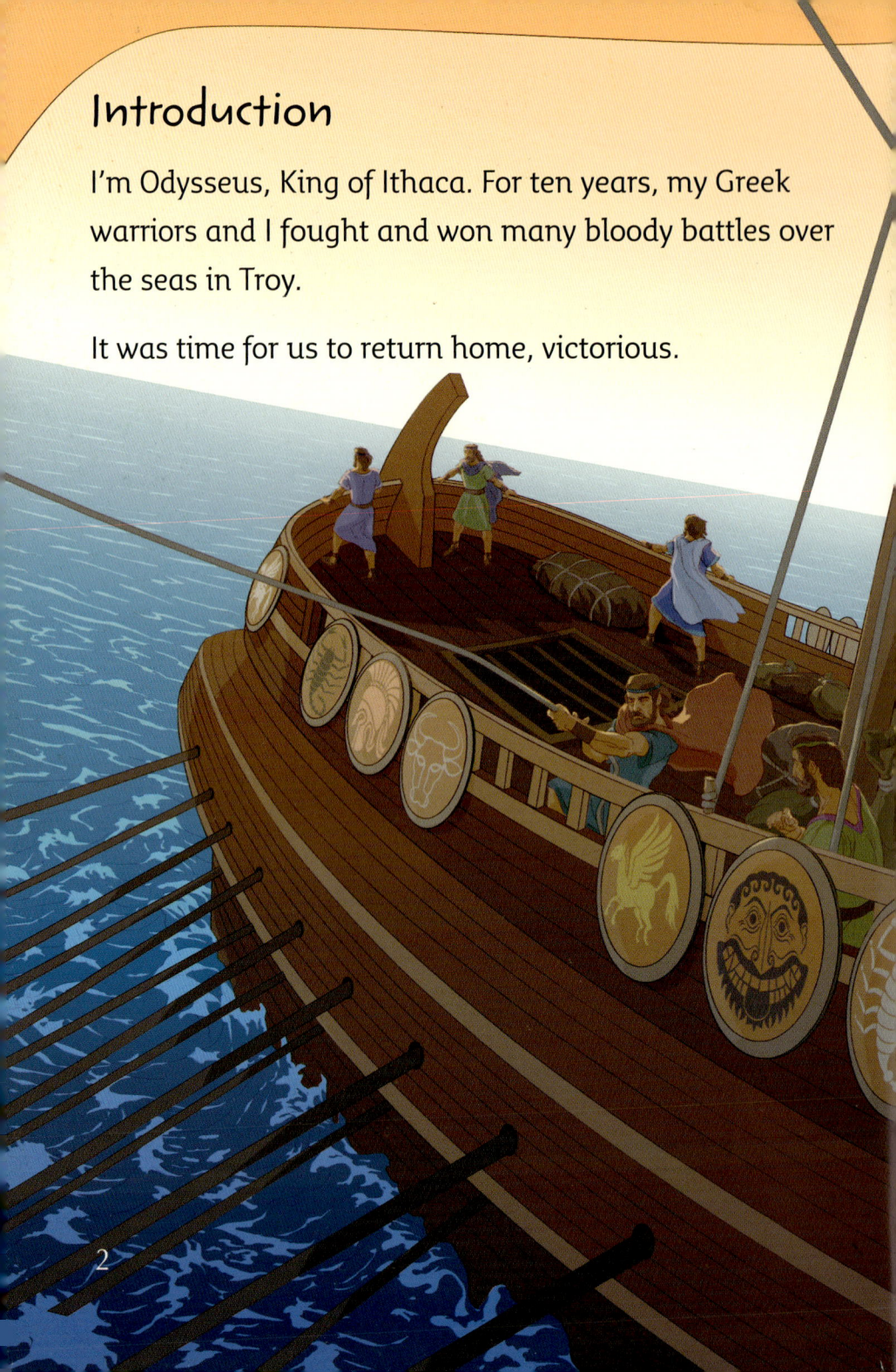

I looked out across the sea towards Ithaca. Home!

I dreamt of holding my beautiful wife Penelope in my arms and kissing my baby. Except Telemachus wasn't a baby any more – he was a ten-year-old boy. What did he know about his father? Did he ever think of me?

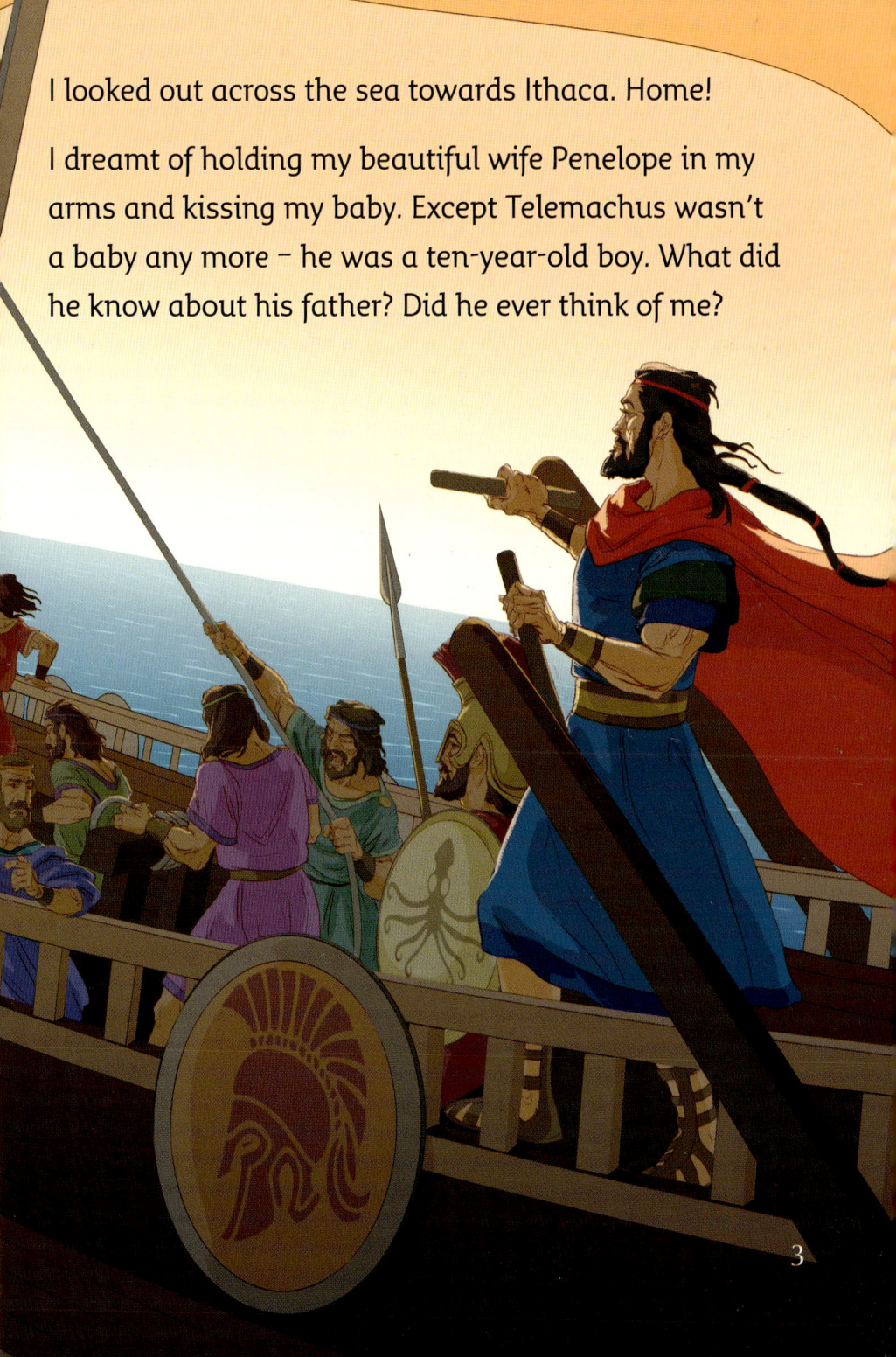

1 The Cyclops

My growling stomach brought my thoughts back to the present. My crew were exhausted after long years of war. We'd been at sea for weeks and we'd run out of food and fresh water. We needed to find land soon or we'd starve, and never see home again.

Suddenly, the lookout cried, "An island!"

We dropped anchor, and collapsed on the beach, weak with hunger and thirst. The sun beat down on our tired bodies. Salty sweat stung my cracked, dry lips.

I lifted my head from the hot sand and caught the delicious scent of cheese and milk on the warm breeze. Food, at last!

We followed the enchanting smell to a large, damp cave. Inside, we gorged on creamy milk, cheese and bread, never once wondering where the feast came from.

As the sun set, a flock of sheep trotted in. As the last sheep entered, a dark shadow fell over the mouth of the cave. Guiltily, we dropped the food and stared open-mouthed as a giant form lumbered into the cold, wet cave.

The Cyclops towered over us. His one bloodshot eye flared, maddened with rage. We cowered behind some rocks.

"Steal my dinner, will you?" he roared. "I'll have *you* for dinner now!"

Sweeping his huge arm, he knocked us to the ground. We ran, desperately trying to reach the open air. But the Cyclops was already there, rolling an enormous stone over the entrance.

We were plunged into darkness.

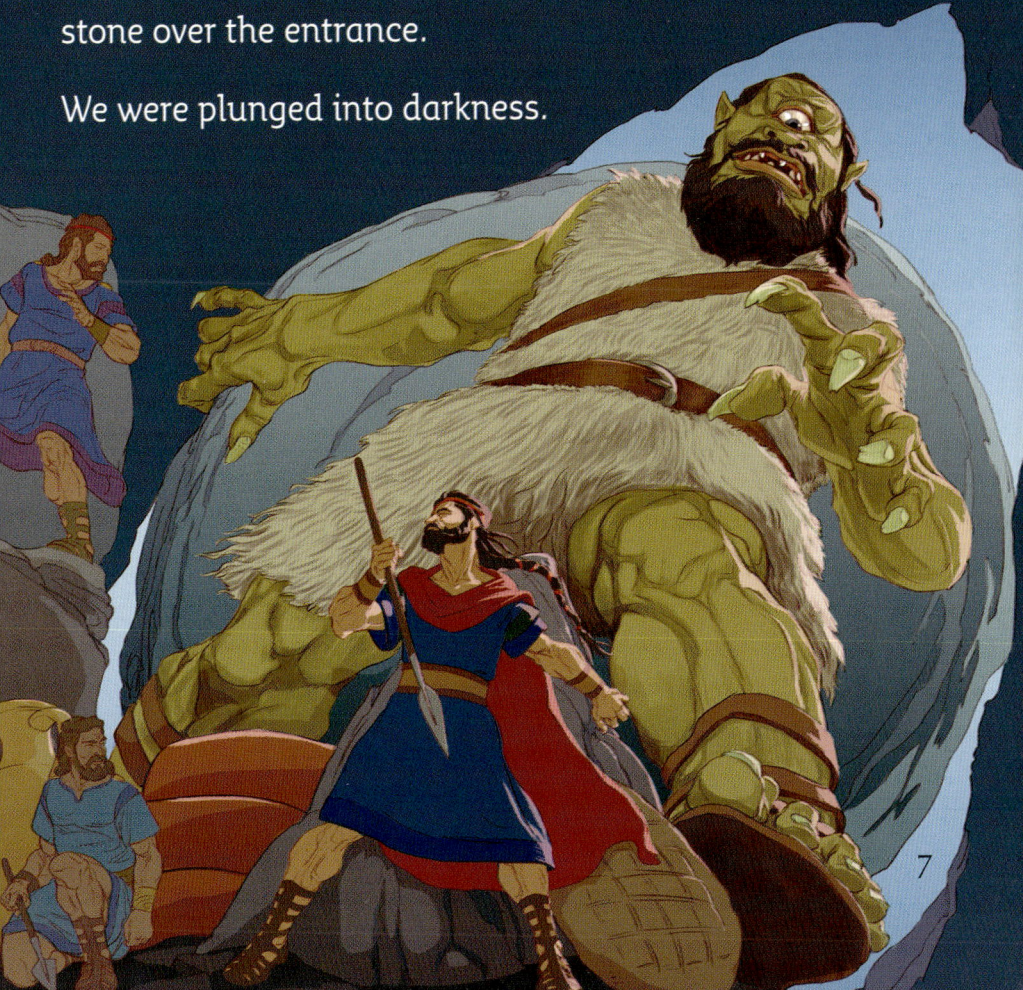

To stay in the cave would mean certain death. Our only chance was to attack. We drove a spear into the Cyclops's only eye, blinding him instantly.

He screamed in agony. "You'll never leave this cave alive," he shrieked, his high-pitched wail echoing off the walls.

The Cyclops stumbled around the cave, trying to find us. His filthy hands groped about amongst the rocks. We dodged him all night long until he finally fell asleep.

We hid in the shadows, afraid to move a muscle, unsure if we'd ever escape …

The sun rose and the Cyclops rolled back the stone. As the sheep filed from the cave, the Cyclops ran his hand over the back of each one, checking we weren't trying to escape.

The Cyclops gave me an idea.

"Quick," I whispered to my men. "Hold on to the underside of the sheep."

We clung desperately to the slippery, oily wool, our hearts beating so loudly I feared the Cyclops would hear.

His large hand patted the sheep I was clinging to. All I could do was hold my breath and hope he wouldn't find me. With my heart in my mouth, I held on tight. I could smell the Cyclops's hot, foul breath.

Then my sheep ran out to the glorious green pastures. Relief!

We dropped from the sheep and ran without a backwards glance. We scrambled on to the ship, lifted the sail and headed out to sea.

The Cyclops stumbled after us. "Poseidon!" he roared from the shore. "Odysseus has blinded me. Seek vengeance for me, your son!"

2 The Sack of Winds

Poseidon, the sea god, had been my deadly enemy since the Trojan wars.

He rose in fury from the waves and silenced the winds. Our sails fell loose and empty, and our ship floated aimlessly on the glassy sea.

Night and day, we rowed and rowed, until our muscles ached and our hands were blistered and bleeding. Through salt-encrusted eyelashes, I gazed out at the endless, flat sea.

From the corner of my eye, I spotted something glinting on the horizon. Floating towards us was an island.

At last, a place to rest. At least, I hoped it was …

As we approached the island, a large palace came into view, its bronze walls glowing in the hot sun.

At the gates, King Aeolus stood with his arms open. "Welcome! Come and rest." We collapsed on the shore, thankful for the king's hospitality.

"In return, all I ask for is a good story. I never leave the island, but I like to hear about the outside world," explained King Aeolus.

I told him our story, of our battles in Troy and our encounter with the Cyclops and Poseidon. We'd been through so much, I wasn't sure my men could take much more.

King Aeolus was captivated by my tale and laughed when he heard of Poseidon's rage.

"Come." He drew me to one side. "I've a gift for you, stolen from our old friend Poseidon," and he handed me a writhing sack. Inside were the four winds: North, South, East and West.

King Aeolus pulled the snaking West Wind out and released it. "This wind will carry you home, Odysseus. Just don't release the other winds unless you need to."

Relief and gratitude washed over me; this was the help we needed to get home.

With the West Wind behind us, we flew across the waves. Ithaca was in sight, its mountains rising proudly above the sea.

Our long journey would soon be over so I decided to rest. The next day I'd be reunited with my family and we'd have a great feast. I could almost taste the fresh, sweet spring water of Ithaca.

I awoke with a start. The ship was being tossed and turned. The winds lashed at the sails and the men shouted, struggling to control the ship.

My captain had opened the sack. The four winds tore upwards and spiralled wildly into the skies, whipping up a huge storm.

"I'm so sorry, Odysseus," the captain stuttered over the deafening roar of the winds. "We thought there was treasure in the sack."

We desperately tried to keep our course for home, but the storm was too strong. We were dragged far off-course, until Ithaca was only a memory once more.

The howling wind and rain battered us, tearing the sails. Crashing waves flooded the deck. We couldn't bail out the water fast enough.

The crew's shoulders drooped in shame as we battled the storm.

"Fools! We were almost home!" Too angry to say any more, I sank to my knees.

3 The Sirens

At last, the storm ended and the sun shone down on us once more. Exhausted, I surveyed my wrecked ship. Part of me wanted to give up, but then I remembered my family. I knew I had to keep going, and I'd need the support of my crew to do it.

I rolled up my sleeves and worked alongside my men repairing the sails.

Suddenly, the sun went behind a cloud and there was a cold, damp feel to the air. Something was waiting nearby and it sent shivers over my body.

I remembered a warning about the Sirens' island. The Sirens were cruel, heartless, winged creatures. Their bewitching song would pull us towards the rocks, and to our deaths.

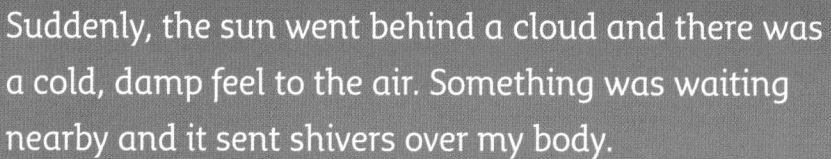

"Quick, men!" I shouted. "We must be approaching the Sirens. Block your ears with wax so you can't hear their deadly song."

I didn't block up my own ears. I ordered my men to tie me tightly to the mast so I couldn't change the course of the ship. I wanted to hear the music, to experience the Sirens' song ... and to survive it.

A beautiful, dreadful song washed over me in waves. It was irresistibly sweet and sad, drawing me in with its enchanting notes. Despite the awful appearance of the Sirens, I longed to go to them. I struggled to free myself from the ropes, cutting my wrists and ankles. I begged my men to sail towards the music. I promised them all the riches in the world if they'd change course.

They looked at me fearfully, but thankfully they couldn't hear my pleas and rowed harder to escape the Sirens.

4 Dragons and whirlpools

Eventually, we drifted to safety, out of reach of the Sirens' song.

I felt empty and exhausted, but I had to find some energy. The sea had begun to swirl and a current was pulling us. A new danger lay around the corner.

Soon we'd pass through a channel. On one side lay Scylla, the six-headed dragon. On the other side lay Charybdis the swallower, a deadly whirlpool.

I addressed my crew: "Up ahead we face a dangerous stretch of water. Charybdis, the whirlpool, will grab our ship in its deadly grasp and suck us to the underworld. We must row with all our might towards the rocky column on the other side, if we're to survive."

I didn't tell them that Scylla awaited us on that rocky column. It was better for them not to know.

The water started to bubble, swirling around the ship. We felt the strong pull, sucking us off course. A terrible growling, hissing noise swarmed around us.

"All men to the oars!" I shouted, and I grabbed the rudder, steering the ship away from the whirlpool.

The sea was filled with the deafening roar of Charybdis. She sucked the bubbling water down until we saw the rocky sea floor, and then she spat the spray high up into the air. One man lost his oar to the current and, in seconds, it was shattered to pieces by the power of the deadly whirlpool.

"Row harder!" I shouted.

The men bowed their heads and rowed with every ounce of energy in their bodies.

I stared through the grey sea mist, searching for danger, but all I could see was the gleaming wet cliffs.

Suddenly, the cold, scaly heads of Scylla darted down from the black, shining rocks towards us. Scylla plucked six of my brave men from their seats so fast they didn't even scream. Their legs writhed in the tight grasp of the dragon's sharp, shark-like teeth. Scylla's strong jaws muffled the men's desperate last cries.

I raised my sword to attack, but the dreadful monster was already sliding back up the rocky column out of reach, its wicked eyes glinting yellow.

With a last hiss, the dragon was gone.

5 Marooned

The crew pulled in their oars and wept for their lost friends. I looked at the six empty places and told myself I'd lost six men but I'd saved the rest of the crew.

The ship was drifting.

I tried to rally the crew. "Men, we need to keep going."

The faces that looked up at me were clouded with distrust.

The lookout shouted, "An island. Let's land and rest."

There was a loud "Aye!" from the crew.

I was overruled.

The sun blazed down on green pastures and grazing cows. A feeling of unease washed over me as I realised this must be the island of the sun god Helios.

I warned the men: "Whatever you do, don't touch the cows. They belong to Helios. Let's just rest a while, then leave."

They turned away from me. I felt very alone. They blamed me for the loss of our friends to Scylla.

As night fell, the wind rose and a great storm blew over the island. We took shelter.

One of the men turned to me. "If we'd listened to you, Odysseus, we'd be out there in this storm."

The storm raged day after day, week after week. I suspected Poseidon: he still wanted his revenge and had marooned us here without food.

I struggled alone through the rain and wind in search of food. There wasn't a single berry anywhere.

As I returned empty-handed, the rain suddenly stopped and the winds disappeared. My heart dropped as I saw the men eating beef. I kicked over the pot, furious with my disobedient crew. Didn't they remember what happened the last time we helped ourselves to food?

"You can starve if you like, Odysseus, but why should we?" shouted my captain. "And look, the storm has ended! The gods *wanted* us to eat this meat."

I shook my head. "I hope you're right. Let's leave while we can."

Back on the ship, the midday sun beat down on us. I scanned the heavens warily, but all I saw was the burning sun in the bright blue sky. The sun grew hotter and hotter until we were all soaked with sweat and our heads throbbed.

Suddenly, the sun seemed to explode and the voice of Helios, the sun god, called out to Zeus, the god of thunder, "Thieves! Villains! Punish them, Zeus!"

Helios wanted revenge for the crew eating his cows …

6 Shipwrecked

A fiery bolt of lightning tore the sky in two. It struck our ship and shattered it into pieces. The sea boiled around our rapidly sinking ship. We jumped free of it just as it sank down to the darkest depths.

I went under the crashing waves once, twice and then, as I came up a third time, I grabbed on to a piece of the ship's shattered mast. My men were calling for help, but it was all I could do to stay afloat myself.

The storm dragged the remains of the ship and those men who were still alive across miles of sea.

I heard a familiar deep roaring sound – no, it couldn't be …

But it was. It was Charybdis, the whirlpool! There was no escape this time. We were pulled towards her swirling centre. I watched my friends being sucked, one by one, to a watery grave. Their screams for help were drowned in the whirlpool's deadly roar.

It was my turn now; the current span me around and pulled me down. I closed my eyes and saw Penelope reach out to me; in my mind I gripped her hand tightly.

I realised I wasn't falling any more and opened my eyes.

I'd grabbed on to a branch overhanging Charybdis. Using all my strength, I pulled myself free from the whirlpool's grasp. I stared down at my friends' faces swirling into darkness.

In a brief moment of calm, I let go of the tree and grabbed a piece of the ship as it floated past. I clung to it, half dead, and closed my eyes.

I awoke with my face on soft white sand, and the sea gently lapping at my feet. A delicate hand pushed back my hair. I opened my eyes to see the nymph Calypso smiling down at me.

For weeks, Calypso nursed me, gently washing my wounds and feeding me sweet honey.

Gradually, my strength returned.

"Never be weak again, Odysseus," Calypso said to me. "Promise to stay here with me for ever and I'll make you immortal."

Every day for seven years, I asked Calypso to let me go home. Every day, she refused and repeated her offer of immortality. Some days, the temptation to say yes was great. Life was so easy here: no fight, no struggle and no work.

But I loved Penelope. I'd choose one single day with my dear wife over an eternity without her, even in this paradise.

Calypso refused to help me, so I worked day and night to build a raft.

At last, I set sail in the direction of Ithaca.

7 The last challenge

I made good progress on my humble raft. The waves carried me swiftly towards home, until Poseidon raised a terrible storm. It tore my raft apart, but I wouldn't let Poseidon beat me this time.

Over three days, I used the last of my strength to swim for home. My muscles burnt and cramped, but I was determined to make it back.

Finally, I felt the soft sand of my own beach under my feet and smelt the sweet air of Ithaca.

The crooked figure of an old man approached me slowly; then stopped a short distance away. He dropped to his knees and said in a trembling voice, "My lord! You've returned!"

"Eumaeus! My most faithful servant, please, don't kneel." I helped him to his feet.

"My lord, you must hurry," he said. "Penelope is being forced to remarry and there is a plot to murder your son, Telemachus."

I decided to disguise myself as a beggar so as to enter the palace unnoticed.

As I approached, I could see that a feast was underway. The noblemen in the hall were competing for Penelope's hand in marriage.

Penelope, as beautiful as ever, stood in front of the men. "If you wish to marry me, you must perform a feat I've only seen my husband Odysseus complete. You must send an arrow through these 12 axes."

The first competitor swaggered up to the axes; then confidently released his arrow. The arrow flew through the first three axes but fell to the floor. He threw down his bow, his cheeks burning red with embarrassment.

The second was a thin, mean-looking man. With narrowed eyes, he shot his arrow. It passed neatly through eight axes before bouncing off the ninth.

One after another, the men tried but failed.

I stepped forward. "My lady, may a humble beggar try?"

The noblemen around the hall laughed and jeered, but Penelope smiled gently and nodded.

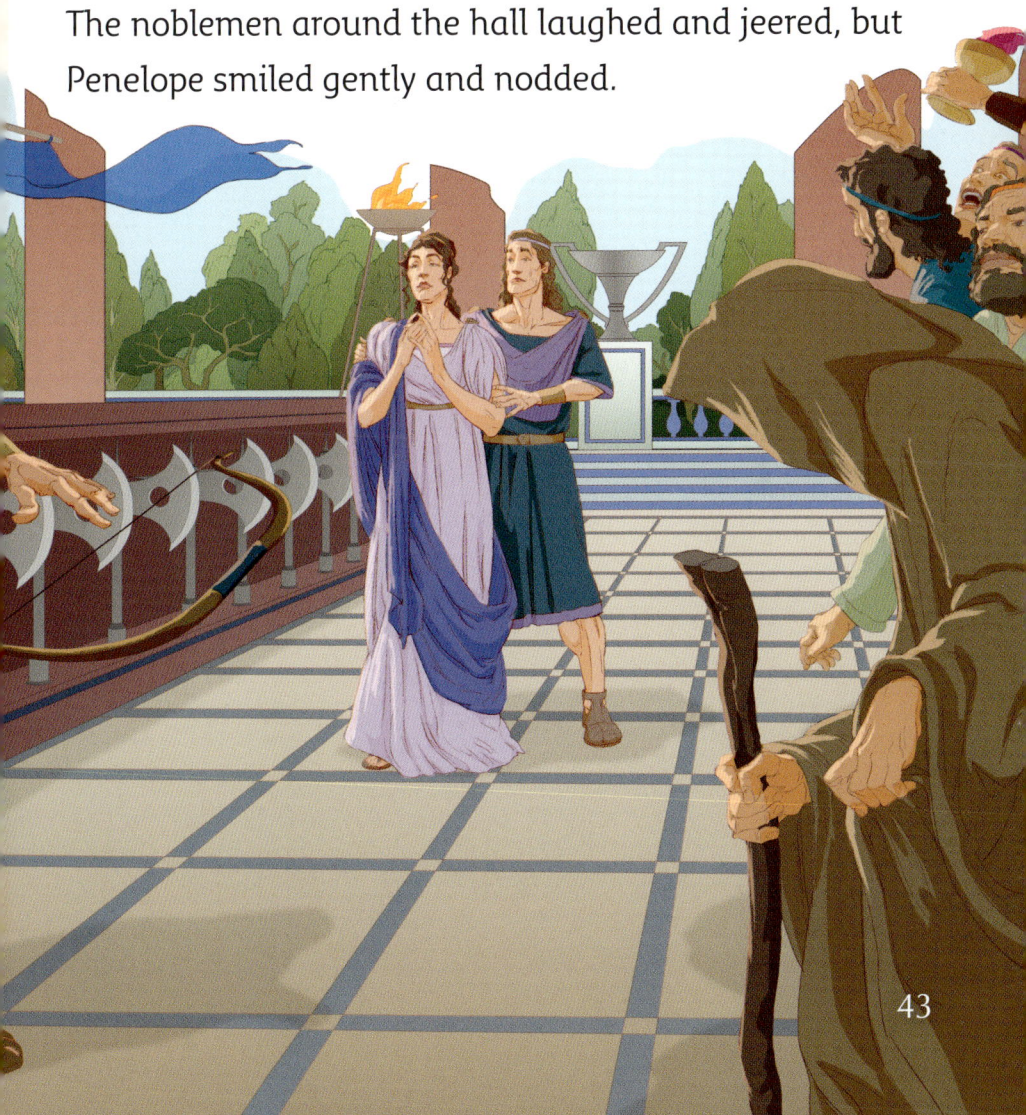

I raised my bow and released the arrow. The arrow quivered, then flew straight through all the axes with a clean whistle. The hall fell silent as the noblemen watched in disbelief.

Penelope looked past my rags and my beard, deep into my eyes.

"Odysseus, can it really be you?" Penelope embraced me.

And there, standing strong behind her, was my boy, Telemachus. We held each other tight. Tears of joy ran down our faces.

In this golden moment, all the trials, hardship and pain of the past 20 years were forgotten. We were reunited at last. I'd finally come home!

Ideas for reading

Written by Clare Dowdall, PhD
Lecturer and Primary Literacy Consultant

Reading objectives:
- identify main ideas drawn from more than one paragraph and summarise ideas
- discuss words and phrases that capture the reader's interest and imagination
- draw inferences and justify these with evidence

Spoken language objectives:
- participate in discussions, presentations, performances, role play, improvisations and debates

Curriculum links: History – ancient Greece

Resources: ICT for research; art materials; pens and papers

Build a context for reading

- Look at the front cover together. Help children to read the name Odysseus. Discuss what they can see and what kind of character Odysseus might be.
- Read the blurb aloud together. Explain that this story is an ancient Greek myth. Ask children about any mythical creatures that they know, e.g. unicorns.
- Establish that mythical creatures are magical beings, with special qualities. Ask children to suggest what kind of mythical creatures Odysseus and his men may meet in this Greek myth.

Understand and apply reading strategies

- Turn to pp2–3. Read the introduction to the children and discuss what is known about Odysseus and how he is feeling.
- Ask children to read Chapter 1 silently, looking for information about the mythical creature.